Tom and Ricky
and the
Birthday Present Mystery

Bob Wright

High
Nova

The Birthday Present Mystery

Bob Wright
AR B.L.: 2.3
Points: 0.5   UG

Cover Design: Nancy Peach
Interior Illustrations: Herb Heidinger
Story: Richard Gold

Glossary: radio, uncle, bakery, block, voices, brother, hotel

International Standard Book Number: 0-87879-397-6

10 09 08 07 06 05 04
15 14 13 12 11 10 09 08

You'll enjoy all the High Noon Books.
Write for a free full list of titles.

Contents

CHAPTER 1

A Chocolate Cake with Candles

It was Saturday. And it was hot. Tom parked his bike in front of Ricky's house. "Ricky, Ricky," he called out.

Ricky opened the door. "Come on in, Tom," Ricky called back.

"I thought we were going to ride our bikes," Tom said.

"We will. We will. Just come in," Ricky said.

"What's up?" Tom asked.

"You'll see," Ricky answered.

Tom walked into the house with Ricky.

"Happy Birthday!" everyone yelled. Even Patches barked.

Tom was surprised. "What's going on?" he asked.

"It's a surprise," Ricky said.

"And did we ever surprise you!" Ann said.

"You sure did," Tom said.

"I hope you like chocolate cake," Ricky's mother said.

"Are you kidding? I love it," Tom said.

Then Ricky's mother brought in a chocolate cake. It had candles on it and it said, "Happy Birthday Tom."

Tom started to blow out the candles.

"Wait. You have to make a wish first," Ann said.

"And did we ever surprise you!" Ann said.

"That's right," Tom said. He didn't do anything. He just looked at the cake. Then he said, "I'm ready."

"OK, then. Blow them out," Ricky said.

Tom blew out all the candles. Then he said, "Come on. Let's all have some."

"I hope you like the cake," Ann said. She started to help cut it.

Ann was a good friend of Tom and Ricky. Sometimes she went bike riding with them.

Then the doorbell rang. "I'll get it," Ricky's mother said. She came back with Mr. Parks. "Look who's here to see you, Tom," she said.

"Mr. Parks! What are you doing here? Who's taking care of your store?" Ricky asked.

"I closed it to come over here. Someone has a present for Tom," he said. Then he gave Tom a big box.

"Who is it from?" Ricky asked.

Tom took off the paper. Then he opened the box. "It's a radio! Thank you Mr. Parks," he said.

"Will you look at that? It can even play tapes," Ricky said.

"That radio is from your Uncle Jack. He asked me to bring it to you," Mr. Parks said.

"That's funny," Tom said.

"What's funny about that?" Ricky asked.

"I don't have an Uncle Jack," Tom said.

"You're kidding," Ricky said.

"No. I mean it," Tom said.

"Can he keep it, Mr. Parks?" Ricky asked.

"He sure can. Someone paid for it. The man said he was your Uncle Jack. He asked me to bring it to you," Mr. Parks said.

"How did he know I would be here?" Tom asked.

"I don't know. But he told me to bring it here for your birthday," Mr. Parks said.

"Maybe he was a good friend," Ann said.

"If the man comes back, I'll find out more. I have to get back to my store now. There might be people waiting to get in," Mr. Parks said.

"I have to get back home. I'll see you later. Happy birthday, Tom," Ann said.

CHAPTER 2

A Radio Robbery

Tom and Ricky rode their bikes into town. They played Tom's new radio.

"That's a good radio," Ricky said.

"It sure is. But I'd like to know who Uncle Jack is," Tom said.

"Maybe someone wanted to surprise you. It might even be your dad," Ricky said.

"It could be," Tom said.

"Come on. Let's buy some tapes for it," Ricky said.

"We can buy them at Mr. Parks' store," Tom said.

They rode down Front Street. Then Tom said, "Look at that. There are a lot of people in front of Mr. Parks' store."

"What's going on?" Ricky asked.

"I don't know. But I see Sergeant Collins there," Tom said.

They stopped their bikes. Then they walked over to Sergeant Collins.

"Is Mr. Parks OK?" Ricky asked.

"He's OK. But his store was robbed," their friend, Sergeant Collins, answered.

"Robbed? When? You must be kidding us," Ricky said.

Then they saw Mr. Parks. "Someone robbed my store. Someone took all my radios," he said.

Tom and Ricky looked around the store. They could see that all the radios were gone. They saw that the back door was open.

Then Ricky asked, "When did the robber take the radios?"

"The robber took them when I was at your house," Mr. Parks said. He was very mad. Then he looked at Tom. "Do you know who took my radios?"

"How would I know?" Tom asked.

"I think someone played a trick on me. I was sent to Ricky's house. I closed my store. Then someone robbed it," Mr. Parks said.

"Do you think I know who took your radios?" Tom asked.

Mr. Parks just looked at Tom.

Then he looked at Tom.
"Do you know who took my radios?"

"Mr. Parks, let me talk to Tom," Sergeant Collins said.

Tom, Ricky, and Sergeant Collins walked away from Mr. Parks.

"Who is Uncle Jack?" the Sergeant asked Tom.

"Why are you asking me that?" Tom asked.

"It was Uncle Jack who wanted Mr. Parks to go to Ricky's house. That's when his store was robbed," the Sergeant said.

"I don't know about Uncle Jack. I don't have an Uncle Jack," Tom said.

CHAPTER 3

Mystery and Mrs. Best

Tom and Ricky left Mr. Parks' Radio Store. They got on their bikes. Patches jumped up when he saw them. He started to bark.

"Come on, Patches," Ricky called.

"Does Sergeant Collins think I took the radios?" Tom asked.

"No. I don't think so. You couldn't have. You were at my house," Ricky said.

"But he was asking me about Uncle Jack, whoever he is," Tom said.

"Sergeant Collins has to find out everything he can. That's why he was asking you questions," Ricky said.

"But who is Uncle Jack? Someone bought that radio," Tom said.

"All we have to do is find Uncle Jack," Ricky said.

"If we only could. But where do we start?" Tom asked.

"I have an idea," Ricky said.

"What is it?" Tom asked.

"Uncle Jack bought a radio, right?" Ricky asked.

"That's right. Someone calling himself my Uncle Jack," Tom answered.

"Uncle Jack asked Mr. Parks to bring the radio to my house. Right?" Ricky asked.

"Right," Tom answered.

"Someone knew Mr. Parks would have to close his store. Someone knew no one would be there. Right?" Ricky asked.

"What's this all about?" Tom asked.

"My mother knew you would be at our house. My mother went to buy the cake," Ricky said.

"That's right. The cake had my name on it," Tom said.

"My mother bought the cake at Mrs. Best's Bakery. Mrs. Best knew it was your birthday," Ricky said.

"She knew I would be at your house," Tom said.

"That's right," Ricky said.

"Now I see what you're saying," Tom said.

"Come on. Let's get over and see Mrs. Best," Ricky said.

"Do you think Mrs. Best robbed Mr. Parks' store?" Tom called out.

"I don't think so. But we need to talk with her," Ricky called back.

"She might know something. She's the only person who knew about the cake and my birthday," Tom said.

Tom and Ricky rode as fast as they could to the bakery. Patches went with them.

"Boy, that smells good," Tom called out.

They could smell good things a block away from the bakery. They stopped their bikes in front. Then they went inside. Patches sat outside. He knew he couldn't go in.

They walked inside. They were the only ones there. There were all kinds of cakes and cookies. Everything smelled so good.

"Where's Mrs. Best?" Tom asked.

"I don't know. She has to be somewhere," Ricky said.

"Did you hear that?" Tom asked.

"What?" Ricky answered.

"I hear two voices. They seem to be in the back room," Tom said.

CHAPTER 4

Voice in the Back Room

Mrs. Best walked into the store from the back room. She was a big lady. She always wore a white dress. She was always happy when she saw Tom and Ricky.

At first, Mrs. Best looked mad. Then she smiled. "Happy birthday, Tom. Did you like your birthday cake? I made that one just for you," she said.

"I sure did like it," Tom said.

"I did, too," Ricky said.

"You two really are growing. I made cakes for both of you when you were little," Mrs. Best said.

Then she smiled. "Happy birthday, Tom."

Tom and Ricky liked Mrs. Best. She was always nice to them.

"Well, what can I do for you?" she asked.

All of a sudden a man yelled from the back room. "What are you doing? I want to get going!"

Mrs. Best didn't look very happy now. She turned to the back room. "Just wait. I'll be right there," she yelled.

"Who's that?" Tom asked.

"That's my brother. He came to see me," she said.

"I didn't know you had any brothers," Ricky said.

"Just this one," she said.

"Does he live in town?" Tom asked.

"No. A long way from here," she said.

"Where are you? I can't wait all day," her brother yelled out.

"I told you to wait," Mrs. Best yelled back.

"I can't wait!" her brother yelled. He went out the back door. Then he banged it closed.

"I'm sorry my brother yelled. He gets that way sometimes. Here's a cookie for each of you. Now what would you like?" she asked.

"There is a mystery," Ricky said.

"A mystery? What kind?" Mrs. Best asked.

"Someone gave me a radio. But I don't know who it is from," Tom said.

"That is a mystery," Mrs. Best said.

"Did you tell anyone that today is Tom's birthday?" Ricky asked.

"No. I didn't tell anyone. But my brother may know something. He has been helping me. He was here when your mother came in a week ago. That's when she told me to bake a chocolate cake for Tom," Mrs. Best said.

"Maybe your brother does know something," Tom said.

"He might. But he just left," she said.

"Do you think we might talk to your brother?" Ricky asked.

"I think you could. He is staying at the old hotel. He does some work there. He gets a free room for the work he does," Mrs. Best said.

"Do you think he's there now?" Ricky asked.

"I'm sure he is there. He always goes back to the hotel. Last week he did a lot of walking up and down Front Street. But today he's mad. So I know he will be at the hotel," Mrs. Best said.

"Come on, Ricky. Let's get going," Tom said.

"Wait. Take this pie to him. He'll like it. It might make him feel better," Mrs. Best said.

"Thanks for the cookies," Tom yelled out.

"I'm glad you liked them," Mrs. Best said.

Then Ricky turned around. "We forgot to ask. What's your brother's name?"

"It's Jack," Mrs. Best called out to them.

CHAPTER 5

The Yellow Door

Tom and Ricky walked out of the bakery. They looked at each other.

"His name is Jack! Did you hear that?" Ricky asked.

"I sure did. Now what do we do?" Tom answered.

"Let's take this pie to Jack. That way we can see what he looks like. Then we can talk with Mr. Parks. We can find out if Jack is the one who bought the radio for you," Ricky said.

"Do you think that Mrs. Best's brother could be that man?" Tom asked.

"He might be," Ricky said.

"Then he could be the man who robbed Mr. Parks' store," Tom said.

"That's right!" Ricky said.

"Mrs. Best is such a nice lady. I hope her brother isn't the robber," Tom said.

"We'll soon find out," Ricky said.

Just then they saw Ann. She was riding down Front Street. Ricky called out to her. "Ann, where are you going?"

Ann stopped her bike. "I'm on my way to King's Market. I have to get some things for my mother. Where are you going?"

Ricky told Ann about Mr. Parks' store.

Then Tom told her about Mrs. Best's brother Jack.

"Have you told Sergeant Collins about all of this?" Ann asked.

"We're going to the hotel first. Then we'll tell Sergeant Collins," Tom said.

"I don't like any of this. It doesn't sound good to me," Ann said.

"Don't worry. We'll be careful," Ricky said. Then Ann left to go to King's Market.

Then Tom and Ricky rode down to the old hotel.

"You wait here in front," Ricky said.

Ricky walked in the hotel with the pie.

The man at the desk asked, "Can I help you?"

"Yes. I'm looking for Jack," Ricky said.

"Jack? Jack? Jack who?" the man asked.

"He does some work for you," Ricky said.

"Oh, yes, that Jack. He does cleaning for us. You have to go around the back. You'll see a yellow door. He lives in back of the hotel," the man said.

Ricky walked out of the hotel.

"Was he there?" Tom asked.

"That man said we have to go around to the back," Ricky said.

They left their bikes in front of the hotel. Then they walked to the back.

There was an old green truck. Then they saw the yellow door. Patches started to bark and run around.

"Patches, be still," Ricky said. Patches sat down.

"You ring the bell," Tom said.

"Why?" Ricky asked.

"You have the pie," Tom said.

"OK," Ricky said. He went up to the yellow door and rang the bell.

No one came to the door.

Ricky rang it again.

Then someone inside yelled, "Who is it?"

"I have something for you," Ricky yelled.

"Go away," the man yelled.

"I have a pie for you. It's from Mrs. Best at the bakery," Ricky called out.

Then the yellow door slowly opened.

"Yes, I'm Jack. What's it to you?"

Tom and Ricky saw a big man. He just stood there looking at Ricky.

"Are you Jack?" Ricky asked.

"Yes, I'm Jack. What's it to you?" Jack asked.

"I have this pie for you," Ricky said.

"What are you looking at? Give me the pie and get out of here," Jack said. He grabbed the pie out of Ricky's hands. Then he banged the door closed.

Ricky walked over to Tom and Patches.

"Boy, he sure was mean looking," Tom said.

"He sure was. But I did get to look inside," Ricky said.

"What did you see?" Tom asked.

"I saw a lot of boxes. They were all over the place," Ricky said.

"Those could be boxes with radios in them," Tom said.

"Now what do we do?" Tom asked.

"Let's go back and see Mr. Parks. Let's tell him what Jack looks like. Maybe Jack and Uncle Jack are the same man," Ricky said.

Tom and Ricky ran to the front of the hotel. They got on their bikes. They were on their way back to Mr. Parks Radio Store.

CHAPTER 6

Jack and Uncle Jack

Tom and Ricky went as fast as they could. Patches was right in back of them. Mr. Parks' store wasn't far from the old hotel. They jumped off their bikes when they got there. Then they ran into the store.

Mr. Parks was busy. He was cleaning up the place. No one else was there.

"Mr. Parks! Mr. Parks!" Tom yelled.

"What is it, boys?" he asked.

"We have to talk with you," Tom said.

"OK. But first I have to say something. I'm sorry I was mad. I didn't mean to be. I know you didn't rob my store," Mr. Parks said.

"That's OK, Mr. Parks. We know you didn't mean to be mad at us," Tom said.

"Now what is it you want to talk about?" Mr. Parks asked.

"Can you tell us what Uncle Jack looked like?" Tom said.

"Let's see. He was big. He was very big. He had dark hair. He looked dirty. And, oh, yes, he had a mark on his right arm," Mr. Parks said.

"That's him! That's him!" Ricky yelled.

"That's Mrs. Best's brother Jack," Tom said.

"Mrs. Best? At the bakery?" Mr. Parks asked.

"Yes! We went to talk with her. We found out she has a brother named Jack. We found out he was there when my mother went to ask Mrs. Best to bake Tom's birthday cake," Ricky said.

"You know what? Mrs. Best's brother does come to town now and then. And every time he's here, something funny goes on in town!" Mr. Parks said.

"Did you ever see him before?" Ricky asked.

"No, I never did. He always stays at the old hotel when he comes back to town. When he gets some money, he leaves," Mr. Parks said.

"How does he get some money?" Tom asked.

"Mrs. Best lets him work a week or two for her," Mr. Parks said.

"This is all adding up," Tom said.

"Wait, boys. This still doesn't mean he robbed my store," Mr. Parks said.

"We went to the old hotel. I looked inside his room when he came to the door of his room. I saw a lot of boxes. They could have radios in them," Ricky said.

"You know what, boys? I think we all better go and see Sergeant Collins," Mr. Parks said.

"I think you're right," Ricky said.

"Let's all go in my car," Mr. Parks said.

They all got in Mr. Parks' car. Then they drove to the police station.

"Does Mrs. Best know about all of this?" Mr. Parks asked.

"No. She just asked us to take a pie to her brother," Ricky said.

"Did you see him at the bakery?" Mr. Parks asked.

"No. He was in the back room. He was yelling at Mrs. Best. Then he left," Tom said.

CHAPTER 7

Caught!

Mr. Parks stopped his car in front of the police station. Tom, Ricky, and Mr. Parks all ran inside. Sergeant Collins saw them coming.

"Hi, everyone. What's up? You all look like you know something," the Sergeant said.

"We think we do. You tell him, Ricky," Mr. Parks said.

Ricky told how he and Tom went to see Mrs. Best. They told about seeing Jack and boxes that might have radios in them.

"Jack could be our man," Sergeant Collins said.

"Don't you think he is?" Tom asked.

"A lot of people are big. A lot of people have dark hair. A lot of men have marks on their arms. But if he has the radios, then he's the robber," Sergeant Collins said.

"Now what do we do?" Mr. Parks asked.

"Let's all get in my car. Let's all go to the hotel," the Sergeant said.

They all went out to Sergeant Collins' car. The hotel was near the police station. Sergeant Collins parked his car in front of the hotel.

"I'll go first," the Sergeant said. Tom, Ricky, and Mr. Parks were right in back of him.

When they got to the back of the hotel, Sergeant Collins called out, "Stop!" Then Tom, Ricky, and Mr. Parks saw Jack. He was putting boxes into the green truck.

Jack stopped. He looked at Sergeant Collins. "I'm not doing anything. I'm just moving my things," he said.

"I'll have to look at those boxes," the Sergeant said.

"What for?" Jack yelled.

Sergeant Collins started to walk over to the boxes in the truck. Then Jack started to run.

"I wouldn't do that. Stop where you are. Don't take another step. I mean it," the Sergeant said.

Jack stopped. Sergeant Collins looked at the boxes. "Come over here, Mr. Parks. These boxes are filled with radios." the Sergeant said.

*"I'll have to look at those boxes,"
the Sergeant said.*

Mr. Parks walked over to the green truck. He looked at the boxes. "These are my radios. I think they're all here," he said.

"You better come with me. We're going down to the police station," Sergeant Collins said to Jack.

"It was those kids. I would have gotten away with this. But they had to bring me that pie!" Jack said.

"Get in the car," the Sergeant said. Then he called out to Mr. Parks, "Can you get all those radios back to the store?"

"We'll help him," Tom called back.

"We might as well use the truck. It's all loaded up," Mr. Parks said.

They all got in the truck and went back to the radio store. Tom and Ricky helped Mr. Parks unload the truck.

Then Mrs. Best walked in. "Sergeant Collins just called me. I'm very sorry, Mr. Parks. Jack needs help. Maybe he'll get some now," Mrs. Best said.

"Don't worry, Mrs. Best. I have all my radios back, thanks to Tom and Ricky," Mr. Parks said.

Then Tom turned to Ricky. "It's getting late. I think we better get back home."

"I think so, too," Ricky said.

"This has been a birthday I'll never forget," Tom said.

"That's right. You got a radio from a mystery uncle," Ricky said.

Then Mr. Parks asked," Do you like that radio, Tom?"

"I sure do," Tom said.

"You have really helped me. I would like to take that radio and give you a better one," Mr. Parks said.

"You're kidding," Tom said.

"No. I mean it," Mr. Parks said.

Mr. Parks took Tom's radio. Then he gave him a better one. "This one has more stations on it. And, Ricky, for you, here are some tapes," Mr. Parks said.

"Thank you!" Ricky said.

Then Mrs. Best said, "And come by my bakery next week. I'll have a chocolate cake that says 'thanks' on it."

Tom and Ricky walked out of the store.

"You know what?" Tom asked.

"What's that?" Ricky asked.

"On my next birthday, let's not have any more surprises!" Tom said.